VILE VISITORS

DIANA WYNNE JONES' first children's book was published in 1973. Her magical, humorous stories have enthralled children and adults ever since, and she has inspired many of today's children's and fantasy authors. Among Diana's best loved books for older children are the *Chrestomanci* series and the *Howl* books. Her novel, *Howl's Moving Castle* was made into an award-winning film. She was described by Neil Gaiman as "the best children's writer of the past 40 years".

Diana Wynne Jones

VILE VISITORS

Illustrated by Marion Lindsay

HarperCollins *Children's Books*

First published in hardback in Great Britain
by HarperCollins *Children's Books* in 2012
HarperCollins *Children's Books* is a division of
HarperCollins*Publishers* Ltd,
77-85 Fulham Palace Road, Hammersmith, London W6 8JB

The HarperCollins *Children's Books* website address is:
www.harpercollins.co.uk

www.dianawynnejones.com

1

ISBN: 978-0-00-748942-8

Printed and bound in Great Britain by
Clays Ltd, St Ives plc

Contents

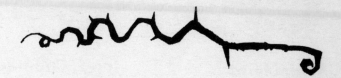

Angus Flint

Tony, Candida and Pip

Pip

Angus driving

Menace

Chair Person

Marcia and Simon

The chair

Mum

Who Got Rid of Angus Flint?

Chapter One

The day my sister Cora went away for a fortnight, a friend of Dad's called Angus Flint rang up out of the blue. He said his wife had just left him, so could he come and see us to cheer himself up? I don't know how my father came to have a friend like Angus Flint. They met at college. One of them must have been different.

Anyway, Dad was pleased Angus Flint had not forgotten him, so he said "Yes," and then told Mum. Mum said "Oh," in the blank sort of way I do when I find my brothers have pinched all my chocolate. Then she said, "I suppose he can have Cora's room." Imagine the way an Ancient Roman might say, "I suppose the lions can have my best friend," and you'll know how she said it.

That ought to have been a warning because Mum can like people no sane person can stand, but I was doing my piano practice, so I didn't pay attention. Miss Hawksmoore had given me an old children's song to work on called *Elfin Dance*, and I wasn't very good at playing it. It sounds like two very glum medium-sized elephants trying to waltz. And the next number in my book is another old song called *The Fairies Party*. I only carry on because I like our piano so much. It's a great, black, grand piano that Mum bought for £100, cheap at £1,000 to our minds.

Chapter One

Pip can't decide what he's a genius *at*, but, a little while ago, he thought he might be a genius at playing the piano. He was doing his practice when Angus Flint arrived. But before that, Pip and Tony – Tony's the brother between me and Pip – had been so glad that Cora was not around to henpeck them that they had celebrated by eating – well, they wouldn't say what they had eaten, but Tony had come out in spots and been sick. Tony has the art of looking bland and vague when any misdeed happens. Mum thought he really was ill. When Angus Flint breezed in, Tony was in a chair in the sitting-room with a bowl on his knees, and Mum was fussing.

Now this shows you what Angus Flint was like. Mum went to shake hands, saying she was sorry we were at sixes and sevens. And she explained that Tony had been taken ill.

Angus Flint said, "Then open the window. *I* don't want to get it." Those were his first words. He was square and stumpy, and he had a blank sort of face with pouty lips. His voice was loud and jolly.

Mum looked rather taken aback, but she slid the big window open a little and told Tony to go to bed. Dad asked Angus Flint to sit down. Angus Flint looked critically at the chairs and then sat in the best one. Dad had just begun to ask him where he was living these days, when he bounced up again.

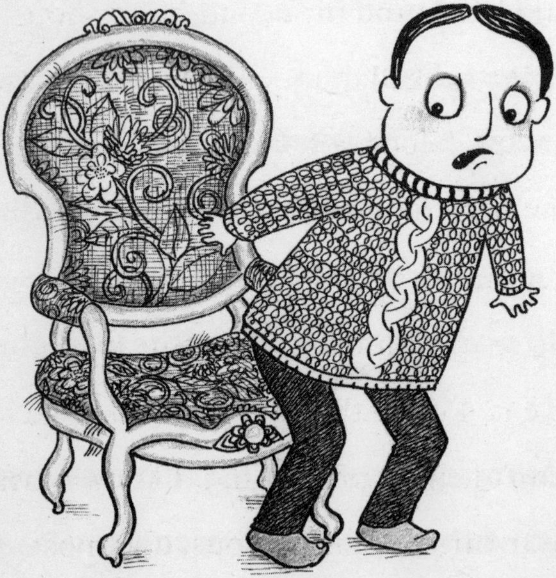

"This is a horribly uncomfortable chair. It's not fit to sit in," he said.

We hadn't done anything to it – though I wish we had now – it was just that the chair is one of Mum's bargains. All our furniture are bargains that Mum has found in second-hand shops. But Pip looked at me meaningfully and grinned, because I was shuddering. I can't bear anyone to insult a piece of furniture to its face. No matter how ugly or uncomfortable a chair or a table is, I don't think it should be told. It can't help it, poor thing. I know most of our furniture is hideous, and most of the chairs hurt you sooner or later, but there's no need to say so. But I don't think furniture can read, so I don't mind writing it.

Meanwhile, Dad had got out of the chair Tony had been sitting in and suggested Angus Flint sat there. "Not that one," Angus Flint said. "That's infested with germs." He ignored all the other chairs and marched over to mine. "I want to sit down," he told me.

"Let Angus have your chair, Candida," Mum said.

I was furious, but I got up. People seem to think children have no rights.

Pip made his sad face at me out of sympathy. Then he spun round on the piano-stool, put his foot down on the loud pedal and slammed into the old song he was learning to play, *How Shall I My True-love Know?* He's only got as far as that one. Tony says he'd know Pip's True-love anywhere: she's tone deaf, with a stutter. She sounds worse with the loud pedal down.

Angus Flint was explaining in his loud jolly voice that he'd taken up Yoga since his wife left him. "You should all do Yoga," he said. "It's very profound. It—" He stopped. Pip's True-love did a booming stutter and made a wrong note. Angus Flint roared, "Stop fooling with that piano, can't you! I'm talking."

"I've got to practise," Pip said.

"Not while I'm here," said Angus Flint. Then, before I could do anything, he sprang up and lifted Pip off the piano-stool by his hair. It hurt Pip a lot – as I found out later for myself – but Pip managed to walk out of the room and not even look as if he were crying. My parents were stunned. They are just far too polite to guests. But I'm not.

"Do that again," I said, "and I shall personally see that you suffer."

All I got from Angus Flint was a blank angry stare, and he went back to my chair. "This is a stupid chair," he said. "It's far too low." The Stare turned out to be his great weapon. He used it on anything he disliked. I kept getting it. Mostly, it was over shutting the window. It's such a big window that, when it's open, it's like having half the sitting-room wall missing. I got colder and colder. I thought Tony's imaginary germs must have gone by now, so I got up and shut it.

Angus Flint did not stop his loud jolly talk to Dad. He just got up and opened it again, talking all the time. I wasn't having that, so I got up and shut it. Angus Flint got up and opened it. I forget how many times we did this. In between, Angus Flint patted Menace. At least – I think he thought he was patting Menace, but Menace had every excuse to think he was being beaten.

"Good little dog, this," Angus Flint kept saying. Clout, thump!

"Don't hit him so hard," I said. I got the Stare again, so I got up and shut the window. While Angus Flint was opening it, Menace saved his ribs from being broken by squeezing under one of the cupboards and staying there. The space was small even for a dachshund.

Chapter Two

Menace didn't even come out from under the cupboard for supper, although it smelt delicious. Mum cooks her best food for visitors.

Mum's turn to be insulted. Angus

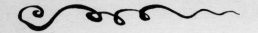

Flint cut off a very small corner of his chops and nibbled it like a rabbit. “This is nice, Margaret!” he said. He sounded thoroughly surprised, as if Mum was famous for cooking fried toads in snail sauce. Then he went on telling Dad that the current government was very profound. Mum was looking stormy and Dad seemed crushed by then. So I told Angus Flint that it wasn’t profound at all. I didn’t see why I shouldn’t. After all, I am going to have the vote one day. But I got the Stare Treatment again, and then Angus Flint said, “I don’t want to listen to childish nonsense.”

I felt almost crushed too. I was glad it was *Celebs Have Talent* on the telly. Pip and I did the washing up in order to see it, and Tony got out of bed – he'd watch that programme if he was dying. We were all crouched around the television, ready to go, when Angus Flint came bustling in from the sitting room where Mum was giving him polite coffee, and turned it over to the other channel. We all yelled at him.

"But you must watch *Girls Galore*," he said. "It's very profound."

Very profound my left fibula! It's one of those awful series about girls sharing a flat. They undress a lot, which accounts for Angus Flint finding it profound. And he stood over the knob, too, so we couldn't turn it back without wrecking the telly. Tony was so furious that he stormed off to fetch Dad, and Pip and I raced after him.

Dad said, "I've had about enough of Angus!" which is strong language from him, and Mum said, "So have I!" and we all thundered back to the dining-room.

And, would you believe this? Angus Flint was standing on his head, doing Yoga, watching *Girls Galore* upside-down! You can't argue with someone who's upside down. We tried, but it just can't be done. Instead of a face, you have to talk to a pair of maroon socks – with a hole in one toe – nodding gently at eye-level. The face you ought to be arguing with is on the floor, squashed and purple-looking and the wrong way up. And when you've talked to the socks for a while, the squashed face on the floor says, "I have to stay like this for ten more

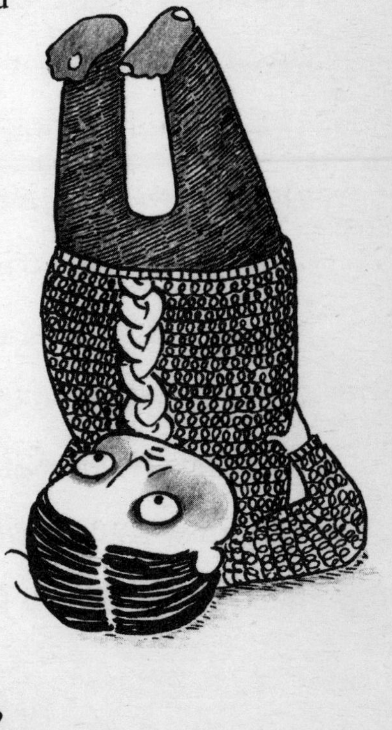

minutes," and you give up and go away. You have to.

We went to bed. I don't know how my parents managed for the rest of the evening, but I can guess. I heard them coming to bed. Dad was most earnestly probing to find out when Angus Flint intended to go. From the strong silence that followed, I gathered that Dad was getting the Stare Treatment too.

In the middle of the night, we were all woken up by a dreadful smell of burning. We thought the house was on fire at first. We were quite pleased, because that's one thing that's never happened to us yet. But the smell turned out to come from the kitchen. It was thick and black, like when you burn toffee.

So we all rushed into the kitchen. Angus Flint was there, calmly stuffing what looked like clean white sheets into the boiler.

"I had to burn these," he said. "They were covered with sugar or something."

"I could have washed them," said Mum.

She got the Stare. "They were ruined," said Angus Flint.

I looked at Pip. He was horribly disappointed. He has always had such

faith in putting sugar in the beds of people he isn't keen on, for a prank. It's supposed to melt and make the victim sticky as well as scratchy. I've told him over and over again that it's worth taking the time to catch fleas off Menace. But I suppose Angus Flint would have burnt the sheets for fleas too.

He went to bed with clean sheets – Mum made his bed, because he never then, or any other time, did a thing for himself – saying he would sleep late next morning. In fact, he got up before I did and ate my breakfast. Dad fled then.

He said he had an urgent experiment at the lab. The coward. He saw me coming. And I couldn't complain to mum either, because Angus Flint took her over and told her all morning how his wife had left him.

We heard quite a lot of it. The story had a sort of chorus which went, "Well, I couldn't stand for that, and I had to pinch her." The chorus came so many times that the poor woman must have been black and blue. No wonder she left him! If I were her, I would have— Well, perhaps not, because, as we were swiftly finding out, Angus Flint was quite immune to anything ordinary people could do.

Mum was tired out by lunch time. “Get lunch, Candida,” she said. “I’m going out. I’ve got the – er – a meeting. I shan’t be in till nearly seven.”

That was how our heartless and cowardly parents left Tony, Pip and me alone all and every day with Angus Flint.

Chapter Three

Of course we objected to being left alone with Angus Flint. Dad said that it was fair shares, because they had him all evening. My mother had the cheek to say to us, “Well, darlings, if you three can't get rid of him, nobody can."

I raved at her. She didn't know what it was like. He took Pip's football away because he said we were making a noise with it. He took all the toy drums, all my new paper, and Tony's trains. Tony has a way of leaving half-made models about, and Angus Flint used to take them apart whenever he came across them. He said they were in the way. When I went to complain, he was standing on his head.

He always stood on his head after he'd done anything like that. He stood on his head after he stole my paper. All

I'd done was to make a bad drawing of Angus Flint standing on his head. He'd no business to look at my private paper anyway. I drew it because I was so mad at the way Angus Flint would keep insulting the furniture. The boys can stick up for themselves, but Cora's bed can't. Angus Flint said it was lumpy and hard. He told the dining-table it was rickety and the chairs they were only fit for scrap. He said the sitting-room furniture ought to be burnt.

Tony said that if he hated our furniture so much, he should leave. He got the Stare. Pip asked Angus Flint every day when he was going, but he only got the Stare too. I knew it was no good telling Angus Flint to stop insulting the furniture, so, whenever he complained, I said, "That's a very profound idea." And got the Stare.

After that, the boys went round calling everything "very profound," from the curtains to our comics. Angus Flint must have felt they had something. All our comics suddenly disappeared. After searching everywhere else, we found them in Cora's room, where Angus Flint had been reading them. I rushed at Angus Flint to complain, and there he was, standing on his head again, maroon socks waving, and his face, squashed and purple, giving me the Stare upside-down at floor level.

"Go away. I've got to do this for five more minutes."

"It looks very profound," I said, but I went away quickly while I was saying it. By that time, I was scared of being picked up by my hair again.

I got picked up by my hair for rescuing Menace. Menace did not appear very often for fear of being patted by Angus Flint. He lurked nervously under cupboards. But one morning he rashly lay down outside the boys' room. Pip and Tony decided that Menace would be able to slide into hiding more easily if he had one of my old roller-skates strapped to his middle.

Menace hated the idea.

I heard him hating it and came to help. There was a lot of shouting, and a good deal more yelping from Menace. Then Angus Flint came pelting out of Cora's room roaring at us to be quiet.

Menace fled. He never let Angus Flint get within a foot of him if he could help it. But the skate stayed. Angus Flint trod on it and shot off downstairs. It

was beautiful. We were all sorry when he stopped on the first landing. Then he came pounding upstairs again shouting, "Whose skate was that?"

I said, "Mine," without thinking.

I was picked up and swung about by my hair. It must have hurt me more than Pip, because I'm heavier.

Still, that put an idea into my sore head. I went and borrowed roller-skates from everyone I knew. I got armfuls. Pip and Tony helped me bring them home in carrier bags. There we laid them out, like you do mouse-poison, in cunning corners. It was an awful nuisance. Kids kept coming to the door saying, "My sister says she lent you my roller-skates, and she's no right to do that because they're mine." But there were quite a few left, even after that.

The result: Pip fell over once, Tony twice, and me three times. Mum and Dad were immune. They said they'd had years of practice. And Angus Flint never said whether he'd fallen over or not. He simply collected all the skates up and threw them in the dustbin. He did it just before the dustmen called, so they were gone before we realised. And kids still keep coming to the door to ask for their skates. I've had to part with most of my nicest things in return.

Tony got picked up by his hair because of the plastic stew. He wanted revenge because Angus Flint kept breaking his models. And Tony hated the way Angus Flint always took one rabbit nibble at his food and then sounded so surprised that it was nice. Tony got as annoyed over that as I did at the way Angus Flint kept insulting the furniture. Mum was furious too. After the third time Angus Flint did it, she took to saying pleasantly, "Arsenic does taste nice." At which Angus Flint always gave the same loud jolly laugh. So I think Mum and Tony put their heads together over the stew.

Tony had collected all the bits of left-over plastic model he could find. You know the things you have left after you've made a model. They look like knobby fishbones. Tony had collected them from everywhere he could think of. Because most of them came from the floor or the backs of cupboards, there was a good deal of grit and fluff and Menace's hair with them too. Mum put the first spoonful of stew on Angus Flint's plate, and while she was dipping for the second spoonful, Tony dumped a great handful of mixed plastic and fluff on top of it. Mum never turned a hair. She just poured gravy over the lot and passed it to Angus Flint.

We all watched breathlessly while he took up a forkful and did his nibble. "This—" he began as usual. Then he found what it was. He spat it out. "Who did this?" he said. He knew it was Tony by instinct. He answered his own question by picking Tony up by his hair and carrying him out of the room.

Mum knocked over her chair and

rushed out after them. But by the time we all got to the hall – we got in one another's way a little – Tony was upstairs running his head under the cold tap. And Angus Flint was – yes, you guessed it! – upside down on the hall carpet.

"I don't want any supper, Margaret," his squashed face said.

Mum said "Good!" to the maroon socks and stormed back to the dining-room.

Chapter Four

Next morning, there was nothing for breakfast. Angus Flint had got up in the night and eaten all the cornflakes and all the milk, and fried himself all the eggs.

Chapter Four

"Why is there no food?" he demanded.

"You ate it all," Mum said.

Angus Flint did not seem to notice how cold she sounded. He just set to work to eat all the bread and marmalade too. He simply did not see how we all hated him. He really enjoyed

staying with us. He kept saying so. Every evening when my parents crawled home to him, he would meet them with a beaming smile. "This is such a friendly household, Margaret," he said. "You've done me a lot of good."

"I think we must be very profound," Pip said drearily.

"I suppose I couldn't live here always?" said Angus Flint.

There was silence. A very profound one.

Pip broke the silence by stumping off to do his practice. By that time, the only time either of us dared practise was when our parents were at home. Angus Flint would not let us touch the piano. If you started, he came and picked you up by your hair. Pip and I got so that we used to dive off the stool and under the piano as soon as we heard a footstep. Pip's True-love, when he did manage to practise playing her song, seemed to have developed a squint as well as a stutter, and as for my song that sounded like gloomy elephants, they had got more like despairing dinosaurs. I kept having to apologise to the piano – not to speak of Miss Hawksmoore.

"You should sell that piano," Angus

Flint said, as Pip started bashing away.

Mum would not hear of it. The piano is her best bargain ever. Not everyone can buy a perfect concert-grand for £100. Besides, she wanted us to learn to play it.

By this time, Angus Flint had stayed with us for nearly a fortnight. Cora was due home in three days, and he still showed no signs of leaving. The boys told him he would have to leave when Cora came back, but all they got was the Stare. My parents both realised that something would have to be done and began to show a little firmness at last. Mum explained – in her special anxious way that she uses when she doesn't want to offend someone – that Cora was coming back soon and would need her room. Dad took to starting everything he said to Angus Flint with "When you leave us—". But Angus Flint took not the slightest bit of notice. It began to dawn on me that he really did intend to stay for good.

I was soon sure of it. He suddenly went all charming. He left me some breakfast for once. He even made his bed, and he was polite all morning. I warned the boys, but they wouldn't believe me. I warned Mum too, when she came back suddenly in the middle of the afternoon, but it was a hot day and she was too tired to listen.

"I only keep buying things if I stay out," she said. "I'd rather face Angus Flint than the Bank Manager."

Too right she kept buying things. That week, she'd bought two hideous three-legged tables for the sitting-room, about eight bookcases, and four rolled-up carpets. We were beginning to look like an old furniture store.

Angus Flint heard Mum come back. He rushed up to her with a jolly smile on his face. "Isn't it a lovely day, Margaret?

What do you say to me taking you and the kids out to tea somewhere?"

Mum agreed like a shot. He hadn't paid for a thing up to then. The boys had visions of ice cream and cream buns. I knew there was a catch in it, but it was just the day for tea out on a lawn somewhere, and I did feel we ought at least to get that out of Angus Flint in return for all our suffering. So we all crammed into his car. Angus Flint drove exactly like you might expect, far too fast. He honked his horn a lot, overtook everything he could – particularly on corners – and he expected old ladies

MDM87N

to leap like deer in order not to be run over. Mum said what about the Copper Kettle? Tony said the cakes in the other place were better. But Angus Flint insisted that he had seen, "A perfect little place," on his way to stay with us.

We drove three times round town looking for the perfect little place, at top speed. Our name was mud in every street by then. We called out whenever we saw a cafe of any kind after a while, but Angus Flint just said, "We can't stop here," and sped on.

After nearly an hour, when Pip was near despair, we ended up roaring through Palham, which is a village about three miles out of town. There was a place called "Ye Olde Tea Shoppe" with striped umbrellas. Our spirit was broken by then. We didn't even mention it. But Angus Flint stopped with a screech of brakes. "This looks like as if it might do," he said.

We all piled out and sat under an umbrella.

"Well, what will you have?" said Angus Flint.

Deep breaths were drawn and cream teas for five were ordered. We all waited, looking forward to cream and cakes. We felt we really deserved our teas.

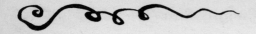

Angus Flint said, "I've applied for a job in your town, Margaret. The interview's tomorrow. Your husband was good enough to say that I could make my home with you. Don't you think that's a good idea?"

We stared. Had Dad said that?

"There's Cora," Mum said. "We've no room."

"That's no problem," Angus Flint said. "You can put the two girls in together."

"No!" I said. If you knew Cora—

"I'd pay," Angus Flint said, joking and trying to be nice. "A nominal sum –

a pound a month, say?"

Mum drew herself up resolutely, to my great relief. "No, Angus. It's absolutely out of the question. You'll have to go as soon as Cora comes back."

Angus Flint did not answer. Instead, he bounced jovially to his feet. "I have to go and see someone for a moment," he said. "I shan't be long. Don't wait for me." And he was back in his car and driving away before any of us could move.

Chapter Five

They brought us five cream teas almost at once. It was a perfect revenge.

Mum could not believe that Angus Flint was not coming back. We ate our cream teas. After a while, Mum let the boys eat Angus's cream tea too, and said we could order another when he came back. When they came with the bill, she said we were expecting a friend, who would pay.

Half an hour later, they began to look at us oddly.

Half an hour after that, they took the umbrellas out of the tables and stood the chairs on them suggestively.

A short while after that, they came and asked to be paid. They made it quite clear that they knew we were trying to cheat them. They refused Mum's desperately offered cheque. We had to go through all our pockets and shake Mum's bag out on the table, and even then we were 2p short. They forgave us that, but grimly. They looked after us unlovingly as we went. Mum nearly sank under the embarrassment.

Then we had to walk home. It was still hot. Tony hates walking, and he whined. Pip got a blister and whined too. Mum snarled and I snapped. We were all in the worst tempers of our lives by the time we plunged up the garden path and burst into the house. We knew that Angus Flint would be standing there, upside-down on the hall carpet, to meet us.

"And this time I shan't care that it's his socks I'm talking to!" I said.

But the person standing in the hall was Dad. He was the right way up, of course, and wondering where we'd all got to. Mum went for him with all her claws out. "Have you had the nerve to tell Angus Flint that he could live with us? If so—" I felt quite sorry for my father. He admitted that, in the heat of the first reunion, he might have said some such thing, but – Oh boy! Never have I heard my mother tell someone off like she did then. I couldn't do it half so well. Even Cora couldn't, the time she played the evil headmistress in the school play.

After that, for a beautiful, peaceful half evening, we thought Angus Flint had gone for good. We kept the window shut, played the piano, watched the things we wanted on the telly, and cheered Dad up by playing cards with him. We were all thoroughly happy, when Angus Flint came back again. He knew we were likely to complain, I suppose, so he brought a girlfriend home with him to make sure we couldn't go for him.

The girlfriend was a complete stranger to us. Hand-picked for her big smile, with glasses and a giggle.

"Teach her to play cards," said Angus Flint. "She's quite clever really."

She wasn't. But neither was Angus Flint, when it came to cards. Have you ever played cards with somebody who thinks for twenty minutes before he puts a card down, and then puts down exactly the wrong one? He played the girl's hand too, though she was slightly better at it than he was. We went to bed after the first game. But Angus Flint didn't take the girlfriend home until well after midnight. I know, because I heard Mum let fly again when he did.

Angus Flint came back at three and

woke me up hammering at the front door.

When I let him in, he said, "Didn't you hear me knocking? I might have caught my death."

I said, "I wish you had!" and escaped into the sitting-room before he could pick me up by my hair.

Menace was there. He crawled nervously out from under the piano to be stroked.

"Menace," I said. "Where's your spirit? Can't you bite Angus Flint?"

Then I thought that I didn't dare bite Angus Flint either, and got so miserable that I went wandering round the room. I patted the uncomfortable chairs and the poor ugly tables, and stroked the piano.

"Chairs," I said, "stand up for yourselves! He insults you all the time. Tables," I said, "he said you ought to be burnt! Piano, he told Mum to sell you. Do something, all of you! Furniture of the world, unite!" I gave them a very stirring speech, all about the rights of oppressed furniture, and it made me feel much better. Not that I thought it would do any good. But I thought it was a very good idea.

Chapter Six

Next morning, Angus Flint ate my breakfast as usual, and Mum and Dad went out together to make friends again. Leaving us alone with Angus Flint, yet again!

Chapter Six

At least there was something, 'very profound' on the telly that afternoon. First I ever knew that racehorses were profound, but it meant twenty minutes' peace. I did some practice. The piano sounded lovely. My song that sounded like dancing elephants was getting better; the elephants had shrunk in size and were beginning to sound like mere dancing tortoises, when the door was torn open. I knew it was Angus Flint and dived for safety.

He was in a very bad temper. I think his horse lost. As I crawled out from under the piano, he sat down at it, grumbling, and started to hammer out a song. I was surprised to see that he knew how to play. But he played very badly. Menace began to whine under his cupboard.

Angus Flint thumped both hands down with a jangle. "This is a horrible piano," he said. "It's got a terrible tone, and it needs tuning."

Rotten slander. I don't blame the piano for getting annoyed. Its curved black rear shuddered. One of its stumpy front legs pawed the ground. Then its lid shut with a clap on Angus Flint's fingers. Now I know why Mum got it for only

£100. Angus Flint dragged his fingers free with such a yell that Pip and Tony came to see what was happening.

By the time they got there, both the new, ugly little tables were stealing towards Angus Flint for a surprise attack, each with their three legs twinkling cautiously over the carpet. Angus Flint saw one out of the corner of his eye and turned to Stare at it. It stood where it was, looking innocent. But the piano-stool spun itself round and tipped him on the floor. I think that was very loyal of the stool, because it must have been the one piece of furniture

Angus Flint had not insulted. And, while Angus Flint was sprawling on the floor, the best chair trundled up and did its best to run him over. He scrambled out of its way with a howl. And the nearest bookcase promptly showered him with books.

While he was trying to get up, the piano lowered its music stand and charged.

I don't blame Angus Flint for being terrified. The piano was gnashing its keys at him and kicking out with its pedals and snorting through the holes in its music-stand. And it went galloping around the room after Angus Flint on its three brass castors like a mad, black bull. The rest of the furniture kept blundering across his path. Tables knocked him this way and that, and chairs herded him into huddles of other chairs. But they always left him a free way to run when the piano charged, so that he had a thoroughly frightening time. They never once tried to hurt the three of us.

I stuffed myself into a corner and admired. That piano was an expert. It would come thundering down on Angus Flint. When he tore off frantically sideways, it stopped short and banged its lid down within inches of his trouser-seat. It could turn and be after him again before you could believe it to be possible. Angus Flint dashed round and round the sitting-room, and the piano thundered after him, and when the boys had to leave the doorway, one of the new bookcases dodged over and stood across it, so that Angus Flint was utterly trapped.

"Do something, can't you!" he kept howling at me, and I only laughed.

The reason the boys had to leave the doorway was that the dining-room table had heard the fun going on and wanted to join in. The trouble was, both its rickety leaves were spread out and it was too wide to get through the dining-room door. It was in the doorway, clattering its feet and banging furiously for help. Tony and Pip took pity on it and took its leaves down. It then scuttled across the hall, nudged aside the bookcase, and dived into the sitting-room after Angus Flint, flapping both leaves like a great angry bird. And it wasn't going to play cat and mouse like the piano. It was out to get Angus Flint. He had some very narrow escapes and howled louder than ever.

I thought the time had come to take the show on the road. I made my way around the walls, with tables and chairs trundling this way and that all around me, and opened the window.

Angus Flint howled out that I was a good girl – which annoyed me – and made for the opening like a bat out of hell. I meant to trip him when he got there. I didn't want him getting too much of a start. But the carpet saved me the trouble by flipping up one of its corners around his feet. He came down on his face, half inside the room and half in the garden. The piano and the dining-table both bore down on him. He scrambled up and bolted. I've never seen anyone run so fast.

The table was after him like a shot, but the piano got its rear castor stuck on the sill. It must be very awkward having to gallop with only one leg at the back.

I went to help it, but the faithful piano-stool and my favourite chair got there first and heaved it free. Then it hunched its wide front part and fairly shot across the garden and out into the road after the flying Angus Flint. The chairs and tables all set out too, bravely bobbling and trundling. Last of all went Menace, barking as if he was doing all the chasing single-handed.

I don't know what the other people in the street thought. The dining-table collided with a lamppost halfway down the street and put itself out of the running. But the piano got up speed wonderfully and was hard on Angus Flint's heels as he shot into the next street. After that, we lost them. We were too busy collecting exhausted tables and chairs, which were strewn all down the street. The piano-stool had only got as far as the garden gate, and my favourite chair broke a castor getting through the window. We had to carry them back to the house. And there was a fair amount of tidying up to do indoors, what with the books, the carpets, and Cora's bed.

Cora's bed, probably the most insulted piece of furniture in the house, must have been frantic to get at Angus Flint too. It had forced itself halfway through the bedroom door and then stuck. We had a terrible job getting it back inside the room. We had just done it, and were wearily trying to mend the dining-table – which has never been the same since – when we heard twanging and clattering noises coming from the sitting-room. We were in time to see the piano come plodding back through the window and put itself in its usual place. It looked tired but satisfied.

"Do you think it's eaten him?" Pip said hopefully.

The piano didn't say. But it hadn't.

Mum and Dad came back and we were all cheerfully having a cup of tea when Angus Flint suddenly came shooting downstairs. We think he climbed up the drainpipe in order not to meet the piano again. I suspect that Cora's bed was rather glad to see him.

"I'm just leaving," Angus Flint said.

It was music to our ears! He went straight out to his car too, carrying his suitcase. We all came out to say polite goodbye – or polite good-riddance, as Tony put it.

"I've had a wonderful time," Angus Flint said. "Here's a football for you, Pip."

And he held out to Pip a flat orange thing. It was Pip's own football, but it was burst. "And this is for you," he said to Tony, handing him a fistful of broken plastic. Then he said to me, "I'm giving you some paper." And he gave me one sheet of my own paper back. One sheet! I'd had a whole new writing pad.

"I do hope Cora's bed bit you," I said sweetly.

Angus Flint gave me the Stare for that, but it wasn't as convincing as usual, somehow. Then he got into his car and drove away. Actually drove away and didn't come back. We cheered.

It's been so peaceful since. Mum wondered whether to sell the new tables, but we wouldn't let her. They are our faithful friends. As for the piano, well, Pip has decided he's going to be a genius at something else instead. His excuse for giving up lessons is that Miss Hawksmoore's false teeth make her spit on his hands when she's teaching him. They do. But the real reason is that he's scared of the piano. I'm not. I love it more than that coward Menace even, and I'm determined to work and work until I've learnt how to play it as it deserves.

Chair Person

Chapter One

What happened to the old striped armchair was Auntie Christa's fault.

The old chair had stood in front of the television for as long as Simon and Marcia could remember. As far as they knew, the cushion at the top had always been tipped sideways and it had never been comfortable to sit in. The seat was too short for Dad and too low for Mum and too high for Simon or Marcia. Its arms were the wrong shape for putting things on. Perhaps that was why there was a coffee-stain on one arm and a blot of ink on the other. There was a sticky brown patch on the seat where Simon and Marcia had once had a fight for the ketchup bottle. Then one evening, the sideways cushion at the top wore out. Whatever the chair was stuffed with began to ooze out in a spiky brown bush.

"The armchair's grown a beard," said Simon.

"It looks as if someone's smashed a hedgehog on it," Marcia said.

Dad stood and looked at it. "Let's get rid of it," he said. "I've never liked it anyway. I tell you what – we can sit the Guy in it on Guy Fawkes night. That will make a really good bonfire."

Marcia thought this was a very good idea. Now she thought about it, she had never liked the chair either. The purple and orange and pale blue stripes on it never seemed to go with anything else in the room. Simon was not so sure.

He always liked things that he *knew*, and he had known that chair all his life. It seemed a shame to burn it on the bonfire. He was glad when Mum objected.

"Oh, you can't throw it out!" Mum said. "It's got such a personality!"

"But it's worn out," said Dad. "It wasn't new when we bought it. We can afford to buy a much nicer one now."

They argued about it, until Simon began to feel sorry for the old chair and even Marcia felt a little guilty about burning a chair that was old enough to have a personality.

"Couldn't we just sell it?" she asked.

"Don't *you* start!" said Dad. "Even the junk shop wouldn't want a mucky old thing like—"

At that moment, Auntie Christa came in. Auntie Christa was not really an auntie, but she liked everyone to call her that. As usual, she came rushing in through the kitchen, carrying three carrier bags and a cardboard box and calling, "Coo-ee! It's me!" When she arrived in the living room, she sank down into the striped armchair and panted, "I just had to come in. I'm on my way to the Community Hall, but my feet are killing me. I've been all afternoon collecting prizes for the party for the Society for Underprivileged Children on Saturday – I must have walked *miles*! But you wouldn't *believe* what *wonderful* prizes people have given me. Just look." She dumped her cardboard box on the arm of the chair – it was the arm with the ink blot – in order to fetch a bright green teddy bear out of one of the carrier bags. She wagged the teddy in their faces. "Isn't he *charming*?"

"So-so," said Dad and Marcia added, "Perhaps he'd look better without the

pink ribbon." Simon and Mum were too polite to say anything.

"And here's such a lovely clockwork train!" Auntie Christa said, plunging the teddy back in the bag and pulling out a broken engine. “Isn’t it exciting? I can’t stay long enough to show you everything – I have to go and see to the music for the Senior Citizens’ Dance in a minute – but I think I’ve just got time to drink a cup of tea.”

“Of course,” Mum said guiltily. “Coming up.” She dashed into the kitchen.

Auntie Christa was good at getting people to do things. She was a very busy lady. Whatever went on at the Community Hall – whether it was a Youth Club Disco, Children’s Fancy Dress competition, Dog Training, Soup for the Homeless or a Jumble Sale – Auntie Christa was sure to be in the midst of it, telling people what to do. She was usually too busy to listen to what other people said. Mum said Auntie Christa was a wonder, but Dad quite often muttered, "Quack-quack-quack," under his breath when Auntie Christa was talking.

"Quack-Quack," Dad murmured as Auntie Christa went on fetching things out of her bags and telling them what good prizes they were. Auntie Christa had just got through all the things in the bags and was turning to the cardboard box on the arm of the chair, when Mum came dashing back with tea and biscuits.

"Tea!" Auntie Christa said. "I can always rely on a cup of tea in this house!"

She turned gladly to take the tea. Behind her, the box slid into the chair.

"Never mind," said Auntie Christa. "I'll show you what's in there in a minute. It will thrill Simon and Marcia – oh, that reminds me! The Africa Aid Coffee Morning has to be moved this Saturday because the Stamp Collectors need the hall. I think we'll have the coffee morning here instead. You can easily manage coffee and cakes for twenty on Saturday, can't you?" she asked Mum. "Marcia and Simon can help you."

"Well—" Mum began, while Dad looked truly dismayed.

"That's settled, then," said Auntie Christa and quickly went on to talk about other things. Dad and Simon and Marcia looked at one another glumly. They knew they were booked to spend Saturday morning handing round cakes and soothing Mum while she fussed. But it was worse than that.

"Now, you'll never guess what's in the box," Auntie Christa said, cheerily passing her cup for more tea. "Suppose we make it a competition. Let's say that whoever guesses wrong has to come and help me with the Underprivileged Children's Society party on Saturday afternoon."

"I think we'll all be busy—" Dad tried to say.

"No refusing!" Auntie Christa cried. "People are so wicked, the way they always try to get out of doing good deeds! You can have one guess each. And I'll give you a clue. Old Mr Pennyfeather gave me the box."

As old Mr Pennyfeather kept the junk

shop, there could have been almost anything in the box. They all thought rather hard.

Simon thought the box had rattled as it tipped. "A tea-set," he guessed.

Marcia thought she had heard the box slosh. "A goldfish in a bowl," she said.

Mum thought of something that might make a nice prize and guessed, "Dolls' house furniture."

Dad thought of the sort of things that were usually in Mr Pennyfeather's shop and said, "Mixed-up jigsaws."

"You're all wrong, of course!" Auntie Christa said while Dad was still speaking. She sprang up and pulled the box back to the arm of the chair. "It's an old-fashioned conjurer's kit. Look. Isn't it thrilling?" She held up a large black top hat with a big shiny blue ball in it. Water – or something – was dripping out of the hat underneath. "Oh dear," Auntie Christa said. "I think the crystal ball must be leaking. It's made quite a puddle in your chair."

Dark liquid was spreading over the seat of the chair, mixing with the old ketchup stain.

"Are you sure you didn't spill your tea?" Dad asked.

Mum gave him a stern look. "Don't worry," she said. "We were going to throw the chair away, anyway. We were just talking about it when you came.

"Oh good!" Auntie Christa said merrily. She rummaged in the box again. "Look, here's the conjurer's wand," she said, bringing out a short white stick wrapped in a string of little flags. "Let's magic the nasty wet away so that I can sit down again." She tapped the puddle in the chair with the stick. "There!"

"The puddle hasn't gone," said Dad.

"I thought you were going to throw the hideous old thing away, anyway," Auntie Christa said crossly. "You should be quite ashamed to invite people for a coffee morning and ask them to sit in a chair like this!"

"Then perhaps," Dad said politely, "you'd like to help us carry the chair outside to the garden shed?"

"I'd love to, of course," Auntie Christa said, hurriedly putting the hat and the stick back into the box and collecting her bags, "but I must dash. I have to speak to the vicar before I see about the music. I'll see you all at the Underprivileged Children's Society party the day after tomorrow at four-thirty sharp. Don't forget!"

This was a thing Simon and Marcia had often noticed about Auntie Christa. Though she was always busy, it was always other people who did the hard work.

Chapter Two

Now Mum had told Auntie Christa they were going to throw the chair away, she wanted to do it at once.

"We'll go and get another one tomorrow after work," she told Dad.

"A nice blue, I think, to go with the curtains. And let's get this one out of the way now. I'm sick of the sight of it."

It took all four of them to carry the chair through the kitchen to the back door, and they knocked most of the kitchen chairs over doing it. For the next half hour they thought they were not going to get it through the back door. It stuck, whichever way they tipped it. Simon was quite upset. It was almost as if the chair was trying to stop them throwing it away. But they got it into the garden in the end. Somehow, as they staggered across the lawn with it, they knocked the top off Mum's new sundial and flattened a rosebush. Then they had to stand it sideways in order to wedge it inside the shed.

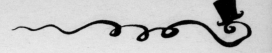

"There," Dad said, slamming the shed door and dusting his hands. "That's out of the way until Guy Fawkes Day."

He was wrong, of course.

The next day, Simon and Marcia had to collect the key from next door and let themselves into the house, because Mum had gone straight from work to meet Dad and buy a new chair. They felt very gloomy being in the empty house. The living room looked queer with an empty space where the chair had been. And both of them kept remembering that they would have to spend Saturday helping in Auntie Christa's schemes.

"Handing round cakes might be fun," Simon said doubtfully.

"But helping with the party won't be," said Marcia. "We'll have to do all the work. Why couldn't one of us have guessed what was in that box?"

"What *are* Underprivileged Children, anyway?" asked Simon.

"I *think*," said Marcia, "that they *may* be the ones who have to let themselves into their houses with a key after school."

They looked at one another. "Do you think we count?" said Simon. "Enough to win a prize, anyway. I wouldn't mind winning that conjuring set. It was a real top hat, even if the crystal ball did leak."

Here they both began to notice a distant thumping noise from somewhere out in the garden. It suddenly felt unsafe being alone in the house.

"It's only next door hanging up pictures again," Marcia said bravely.

But when they went rather timidly to listen at the back door, the noise was definitely coming from the garden shed.

"It's next door's dog got shut in the

shed again," Simon said. It was his turn to be brave. Marcia was scared of next door's dog. She hung back while Simon marched over the lawn and tugged and pulled until he got the shed door open.

It was not a dog. There was a person standing inside the shed. The person stood and stared at them with his little head on one side. His little fat arms waved about as if he was not sure what to do with them. He breathed in heavy snorts and gasps as if he was not sure how to breathe.

"Er, hn hm," he said as if he was not sure how to speak either. "I appear to have been shut in your shed."

"Oh – *sorry*!" Simon said, wondering how it had happened.

The person bowed, in a crawlingly humble way. "I – hn hm – am the one who is snuffle sorry," he said. "I have made – hn hm – you come all the way here to let me out." He walked out of the shed, swaying from foot to foot.

Simon backed away, wondering if the person walked like that because he had no shoes on. He was a solid, plump person with wide, hairy legs. He was wearing a most peculiar striped one-piece suit that only came to his knees.

Chapter Two

Marcia backed away behind Simon, staring at the person's stripy arms. He waved them about in a feeble way as he walked. There was a blot of ink on one arm and what looked like a coffee stain on the other. Marcia's eyes went to the person's plump striped stomach. As he came out into the light, she could see that the stripes were sky-blue, orange and purple. There was a damp patch down the middle and a dark sticky place that could have been ketchup, once. Her eyes went up to his sideways face. There was a beard on the person's chin that looked rather as if someone had smashed a hedgehog on it.

"Who *are* you?" she said.

The person stood still. His arms waved like seaweed in a current. "Er, hn hm, I am Chair Person," he said. His sideways face looked pleased and rather smug about it.

Marcia and Simon of course both felt awful about it. He was the armchair.

They had put him in the shed ready to go on the bonfire. Now he was alive. They hoped very much that Chair Person did not know that they had meant to burn him.

"Won't you come inside?" Simon said politely.

"That is *very* kind of you," Chair Person said, crawlingly humble again. "I – hn hm snuffle – hope that won't be too much trouble."

"Not at all!" they both said heartily.

They went towards the house. Crossing the lawn was quite difficult, because Chair Person did not seem to have learnt to walk straight yet, and he talked all the time. "I believe I am – hn hm – Chair Person," he said, crashing into what was left of the sundial and knocking it down, "because I think I am. Snuffle. Oh dear, I appear to have destroyed your stone pillar."

"Not to worry," Marcia said kindly. "It was broken last night when we – I mean, it was broken anyway."

"Then – hn hm – as I was saying," Chair Person said, veering the other way, "that this is what snuffle wise men say. A person who thinks is a Person." He cannoned into the apple tree. Most of the apples Dad had meant to pick that weekend came showering and bouncing down on to the grass. "Oh dear," said Chair Person. "I appear to have loosened your fruit."

"That's all right," Simon and Marcia said politely. But since Chair Person, in spite of seeming so humble, did not seem very sorry about the apples and just went on talking and weaving about, they each took hold of one of his waving arms and guided him to the back door.

"Only the finest snuffle apples," said Chair Person as he bashed into both sides of the back door, "from the finest – hn hm – orchards go into Smith's Family Apple Pies. This is one of many snuffle facts I know. Er, hm, very few people have watched as much television as I have," he added, knocking over the nearest kitchen chair.

Marcia picked the chair up, thinking of the many, many times she had gone out of the living room and forgotten to turn the television off. Chair Person, when he was an armchair, must have watched hours of commercials and hundreds of films.

Simon turned Chair Person round and sat him in the kitchen chair. Chair

Person went very humble and grateful. "You are – hn hm – treating me with such kindness," he said, "and I am going to cause you a lot of snuffle trouble. I appear to need something to eat. I am not sure what to do about it. Do I – hn hm – eat *you*?"

"We'll find you something to eat," Simon said quickly.

"Eating people is wrong," Marcia explained.

They hurried to find some food. A tin of spaghetti seemed easiest, because they both knew how to do that. Simon opened the tin and Marcia put it in a saucepan with the gas very high to get the spaghetti hot as soon as possible. Both of them cast nervous looks at Chair Person in case he tried to eat one of them. But Chair Person sat where he was, waving his arms gently. "Hn hm, Spiggley's tasty snacks," he said. "Sunshine poured from a tin." When Marcia put the steaming plateful in front of him and Simon laid a spoon and a fork on either side of it, Chair Person went on sitting and staring.

"You can eat it," Simon said kindly.

"Er, hn hm," Chair Person said. "But this is not a complete meal. I shall have to trouble you for a napkin and salt and pepper. And I think people usually snuffle eat by candle light with soft music in the background."

They hurried to find him the salt, the pepper mill and a paper towel. Simon fetched the radio and turned it on. It was playing Country and Western, but Simon turned it down very low and hoped it would do. He felt so sorry for Chair Person that he wanted to please him. Marcia ran upstairs and found the candlesticks from Mum's dressing table and two red candles from last Christmas. She felt so guilty about Chair

Person that she wanted to please him as much as Simon did.

Chair Person was very humble and grateful. While he told them how kind they were being, he picked up the pepper mill and began solemnly grinding pepper over the spaghetti. "Er, hn hm, with respect to you two fine kind people," he said as he ground, "eating people is a time-honoured custom."

Simon and Marcia quickly got to the other side of the table. But Chair Person only took the fork and raked the spaghetti into a new heap, and ground more pepper over that. "There were tribes in South snuffle America," he said, "who believed it was quite correct to – hn hm – eat their grandparents. I have a question. Is Spiggley's another word for spaghetti?"

"No," said Marcia. "It's a name."

Chair Person raked the spaghetti into a different-shaped heap and went on grinding pepper over it. "When the snuffle grandparents were dead," he said, "they cooked the grandparents and the whole tribe had a feast."

Marcia remembered seeing something like this on television. "I watched that programme too," she said.

"You – hn hm – will not know this," Chair Person said, raking the spaghetti into another new shape and grinding another cloud of pepper over it. "Only the sons and daughters of the dead men were allowed to eat the brains." This time he spread the spaghetti flat and ground pepper very carefully over every part of it. "This was so that snuffle the wisdom of the dead man could be passed on to his family," he said.

By this time the spaghetti was grey. Simon and Marcia could not take their eyes off it. It must have been hot as fire by then. They kept expecting Chair

Person to sneeze, since he seemed to have trouble breathing anyway, but he just went on grinding pepper and explaining about cannibals.

Simon wondered if Chair Person perhaps did not know how to eat. "You're supposed to put the spaghetti in your mouth," he said.

Chair Person held up the pepper mill and shook it. It was empty. So he put it down at last and picked up the spoon. He did seem to know how to eat, but he did it very badly, snuffling and snorting, with ends dangling out of his mouth. Grey juice dripped through his

smashed-hedgehog beard and ran down his striped front. But the pepper did not seem to worry him at all. Simon was thinking that maybe Chair Person did not have taste buds like other people, when the back door opened and Mum and Dad came in.

"What happened to the rest of the sundial?" said Mum. "I leave you alone just for—" She saw Chair Person and stared.

"What have you kids done to those apples?" Dad began. Then he saw Chair Person and stared too.

Chapter Three

Both Simon and Marcia had had a sort of hope that Chair Person would vanish when Mum and Dad came home, or at least turn back into an armchair. But nothing of the sort happened. Chair

Person stood up and bowed.

"Er, hn hm," he said. "I am Chair Person. Good snuffle evening."

Mum's eyes darted to the ink blot on Chair Person's waving sleeve, then to the coffee stain, and then on to the damp smear on his front. She turned and dashed away into the garden.

Chair Person's arms waved like someone conducting an orchestra. "I am the one causing you all this trouble with your apples," he said, in his most crawlingly humble way. "You are so kind to – hn hm – forgive me so quickly."

Dad could clearly not think what

to say. After gulping a little, he said in a social sort of way, "Staying in the neighbourhood, are you?"

Here Mum came dashing back indoors. "The old chair's not in the shed any more," she said. "Do you think he *might* be—?"

Chair Person turned to her. His arms waved as if he was a conductor expecting Mum to start singing. "Your – hn hm – husband has just made me a very kind offer," he said. "I shall be delighted to stay in this house."

"I—" Dad began.

"Er, hn hm, needless to say snuffle,"

said Chair Person, "I shall not cause you more trouble than I have to. Nothing more than – hn hm – a good bed and a television set in my room."

"Oh," said Mum. It was clear she could not think of what to say either. "Well, er, I see you've had some supper—"

"Er, hn hm, most kind," said Chair Person. "I would love to have some supper as soon as possible. In the meantime a snuffle flask of wine would be most – hn hm – welcome. I appear to have a raging thirst."

Marcia and Simon were not surprised Chair Person was thirsty after all that pepper. They got him a carton of orange juice and a jug of water before they all hurried away to put a camp bed in Simon's room and make Marcia's bedroom ready for Chair Person. Marcia could see that Mum and Dad both had the same kind of dazed, guilty feelings about Chair Person that she had. Neither of them quite believed he was really their old armchair, but Mum put clean sheets on the bed and Dad carried the television up to Marcia's room. Chair Person seemed to get people that way.

When they came downstairs, the fridge door was open and the table

was covered with empty orange juice cartons.

"I – hn hm – appear to have drunk all your orange juice," Chair Person said. "But I would be willing to drink lemon squash instead. I happen snuffle to know that it has added glucose which puts pep into the poorest parts."

He sat at the table and slurped lemon squash while Marcia helped Mum get supper. Simon went to look for Dad, who was hiding behind a newspaper in the living room. "Did you buy a new armchair?" Simon asked.

"Yes," said Dad. "Hush. That thing in

the kitchen might get jealous."

"So you *do* believe he is the armchair!" Simon said.

"I don't *know*!" Dad groaned.

"I think he is," Simon said. "I'm quite sorry for him. It must be hard to suddenly start being a person. I expect he'll learn to speak and breathe and behave like a real person quite soon."

"I hope you're right," said Dad. "If he just learns to stop waving his arms in that spooky way I shall be quite pleased."

For supper, Chair Person ate five pizzas and six helpings of chips. In between, he waved his arms and explained, "I – hn hm – have a large appetite for my size, though I do not always need to snuffle eat. I am strange that way. Could I trouble you for some Mannings' fruity brown sauce? I appear to have eaten all your ketchup. I think I shall enjoy my – hn hm – life with you here. I suggest that tomorrow we go on – hn hm – a short tour of Wales. I think I should go to snuffle Snowdon and then down a coalmine."

"I'm sorry —" Dad began.

"Er, hn hm, Scotland then," said Chair Person. "Or would you rather charter an aeroplane and take me to France?"

"We can't go anywhere tomorrow," Mum said firmly. "There's Auntie Christa's party in the evening and the coffee morning for Africa Aid before that."

Chair Person did not seem at all disappointed. He said, "I shall enjoy that. I happen to – hn hm – know a great deal about Africa. At the end of the day it must be snuffle said that not nearly enough is being done to help Africa and the Third World. Why, in Kenya alone..." And he was talking almost word for word – apart from the snuffles – the way last night's television programme on

Africa had talked.

Before long, Simon and Marcia had both had enough. They tiptoed away to Simon's room and went to bed early.

"I suppose he's here for good," Simon said.

"He hasn't any other home," Marcia said, wriggling her way into the uncomfortable camp bed. "And he *has* lived here for years in a sort of way. Do you think it was the stuff that dripped from the crystal ball that brought him alive? Or Auntie Christa tapping him with the wand? Or both?"

"Perhaps she could look after him,"

Simon said hopefully. "She does charity and good works. Someone's going to have to teach him all the things that aren't on television."

They could hear Chair Person's voice droning away downstairs. It was a loud voice, with a bleat and a bray to it, like a cow with a bad cold. After an hour or so, it was clear that Mum and Dad could not stand any more of it either. Simon and Marcia heard them coming to bed early too. They heard Chair Person blundering upstairs after them.

"Er, hn hm – oh dear!" his voice brayed. "I appear to have broken this small table."

After that there was a lot of confused moving about and then the sound of running water. Chair Person's voice bleated out again. "Tell me – er, hn hm – is the water supposed to run all over the bathroom floor?"

They heard Mum hurry to the bathroom and turn the taps off. "There are such a lot of things he doesn't know," Marcia said sleepily.

"He'll learn. He'll be better tomorrow," Simon said.

They went to sleep then. There was the first frost of winter that night. They woke up much earlier than they had hoped because it was so cold. Their blankets somehow seemed far too thin and there was white frost on the inside of the bedroom window. They stared at it, with their teeth chattering.

"I've never seen that before," said Simon.

"It's all feathery. It would be pretty if it wasn't so cold," said Marcia.

As she said it, they heard Dad shouting from the bathroom. "What the devil has happened to the heating boiler? It's gone *out*!"

Chair Person's feet blundered in the passage. "Er, hn hm, I appeared to get very cold in the night," his voice brayed. "But I happen to know a lot about snuffle technology. I adjusted the boiler. High speed gas for warmth and snuffle efficiency."

"It's not gas, it's *oil*!" Dad roared. "You turned the whole system off, you fool!"

"Oil?" said Chair Person, not in the least worried. "Liquid engineering. I happen to know – hn hm – that both oil and gas come from the North Sea, where giant oil rigs —"

Dad made a sort of gargling noise. His feet hammered away downstairs. There were a few clangs and a clank and the sound of Dad swearing. After a while the house started to get warm again. The frost on the window slid away to the corners and turned to water.

Marcia looked at Simon. She wanted

to say that Simon was the one who had said Chair Person would be better today. But she could see Simon knew he was just the same. "Do you still think he'll learn?" she said.

"I *think* so," said Simon, though he knew he was going to have to work quite hard to go on feeling sorry for Chair Person at this rate.

Chapter Four

Chair Person ate four boiled eggs and half a packet of shredded wheat for breakfast. He drank what was left of the milk with loud slurping sounds while he told them about oil rigs and then about ship-building. "Er, hn hm," he said. "Studies at the dockyards reveal that less than ten snuffle slurp per cent of ships now being built are named after the Queen. Oh dear, I appear to have drunk all your – hn hm – milk."

Dad jumped up. "I'll buy more milk," he said. "Give me a list of all the other things you want for the coffee morning and I'll buy them too."

"Coward!" Mum said bitterly when Dad had gone off with orders to buy ten cake-mixes, milk and biscuits. She was in a great fuss. She told Chair Person to go upstairs and watch television. Chair

Person went crawlingly humble and went away saying he knew he was – hn hm – being a lot of trouble. "And I hope he stays there!" said Mum. She made Simon help in the kitchen and told Marcia to find twenty chairs – which were all the chairs in the house – and put them in a circle in the living room. "And then I suppose it's too much to hope that Auntie Christa will come in and help!" Mum added.

It *was* too much to hope. Auntie Christa did turn up. She put her head round the back door as Simon was fetching the sixth tray of cakes out of the oven. "I won't interrupt," she said merrily. "I have to dash down to the Community Hall. Don't forget you're all helping with the party this evening." And away she went and did not come back until Mum and Simon had heaped cakes on ten plates and Dad and Marcia were counting coffee cups. "You *have* done well!" Auntie Christa said. "We must have Africa Aid here every week."

Dad started to groan, and then stopped, with a thoughtful look on his face.

The doorbell began ringing. A lot of respectable elderly ladies arrived, and one or two respectable elderly men, and then the Vicar. They each took one of the twenty seats and chatted politely while Simon and Marcia went round with cakes and biscuits and Mum handed out coffee. When everyone had a cup and a plate of something, the Vicar cleared his throat – a bit like Chair Person but nothing like so loudly.

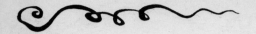

"Er, hm," he said. "I think we should start."

The door opened just then and Dad ushered in Chair Person.

"Oh *no*!" said Mum, looking daggers at Dad.

Chair Person stood, pawing at the air, and looked round the respectable people in a very satisfied way. He had found Dad's best shiny brown shoes to wear and Simon's football socks, which looked decidedly odd with his striped suit. The respectable people stared, at the shoes, the socks, the hairy legs above that, at the stain on his striped stomach and then at the smashed-hedgehog beard. Even Auntie Christa stopped talking and looked a little dazed.

"Er, hn hm," brayed Chair Person twice as loudly as the Vicar. "I am – hn snuffle – Chair Person. How kind of you all to come and – hn hm – meet me. These good people–" He nodded and waved arms at Dad and Mum –"have been honoured to put up with me, but they are only small stupid people who do not matter."

The slightly smug smile on Dad's face vanished at this.

"I shall – hn hm – talk to people who matter," said Chair Person. He lumbered across the room, bumping into everything he passed. Ladies hastily got coffee cups out of his way. He stopped in front of the Vicar and breathed heavily. "Could I trouble you to move?" he said.

"Eh?" said the Vicar. "Er—"

"Er, hn hm, you appear to be sitting in my seat," said Chair Person. "I am Chair Person. I am the one who shall talk to – hn hm – the Government. I shall be running this meeting."

The Vicar got out of the chair as if it had scalded him and backed away. Chair Person sat himself down and looked solemnly round.

"Coffee," he said. "Er, hn hm, cakes. While the rest of the world starves."

Everyone shifted and looked uncomfortably at their cups.

In the silence, Chair Person looked

at Mum. "Hn hm," he said. "Maybe you have not noticed that you've not given me – hn hm – coffee or cakes."

"Is *that* what you meant?" said Mum. "I thought that after all the breakfast you ate—"

"I meant – hn hm – that we are here to feast and prove that we at least have enough to eat," said Chair Person. While Mum was angrily pouring coffee into the cracked cup that was the last one in the cupboard, he turned to the nearest lady. "I decided to grow a beard," he said, "to show I am – hn hm – important. It makes my face look snuffle grand."

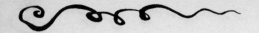

The lady stared at him. Auntie Christa said loudly, "We are here to talk about Africa, Mr Chair Person."

"Er, hn hm," said Chair Person. "I happen to know a lot about Africa. The Government should act to make sure that the African – hn hm – elephant does not die out."

"We were not going to talk about elephants," the Vicar said faintly.

"The snuffle gorilla is an endangered animal too," said Chair Person. "And the herds of – hn hm – wildebeest are not what they were in the days of Dr Livingstone, I presume. Drought afflicts many animals – I appear to have drunk all my coffee – and famine is poised to strike." And he went on talking, mixing up about six different television programmes as he talked. The Vicar soon gave up trying to interrupt, but Auntie Christa kept trying to talk too. Every time she began, Chair Person went, "ER, HN HM!" so loudly that he drowned her out, and took no notice of anything she said. Marcia could not help thinking that Chair Person must have stood in the living room picking up hints from Auntie Christa for years. Now he was better at not letting other people talk than Auntie Christa was.

In the meantime, Chair Person kept eating cakes and asking for more coffee. The respectable people, in a dazed sort of way, tried to keep up with Chair Person, which meant that Simon and Marcia were kept very busy carrying cups and plates. In the kitchen Mum was baking and boiling the kettle nonstop, while Dad grimly undid packets and mixed cake-mix after cake-mix.

By this time Simon was finding it hard to be sorry for Chair Person at all. "I didn't know you thought you were so important," he said as he brought Chair

Person another plate of steaming buns.

"This must be – hn hm – reported to Downing Street," Chair Person told the meeting, and he interrupted himself to say to Simon, "That is because I – er, hn hm – always take care to be polite to people like you who don't snuffle count... I shall make you feel good by praising these cakes. They are snuffle country soft and almost as mother used to make." And turning back to the dazed meeting, he said, "Ever since the days of the Pharaohs – hn hm – Egypt has been a place of snuffle mystery and romance."

There seemed nothing that would

ever stop him. Then the doorbell rang. Unfortunately, Dad, Mum, Marcia and Simon were all in the kitchen when it rang, pouring the last of the cake-mix into paper cases. By the time Marcia and Dad got to the front door, Chair Person had got there first and opened it.

Two men were standing outside holding a new armchair. It was a nice armchair, a nice plain blue, with a pleasant look on the cushion where Chair Person's face had come from. Marcia thought Mum and Dad had chosen well.

"I – er, hn hm – I said take that thing

away," Chair Person told the men. "This house is not big enough for snuffle both of us. The post is – hn hm – filled. There has been a mistake."

"Are you sure? This is the right address," one of the men said.

Dad pushed Chair Person angrily aside. "Mind your own business!" he said. "No, there's no mistake. Bring that chair inside."

Chair Person folded his waving arms. "Er, hn hm. My rival enters this house over my dead body," he said. "This thing is bigger than snuffle both of us."

While they argued, Auntie Christa was leading the coffee morning people in a rush to escape through the kitchen and out of the back door. "I do think," the Vicar said kindly to Mum as he scampered past, "that your eccentric uncle would be far happier in a Home, you know."

Mum waited until the last person had hurried through the back door. Then she burst into tears. Simon did not know what to do. He stood staring at her. "A Home!" Mum wept. "I'm the one who'll be in a Home if someone doesn't *do* something!"

Chapter Five

Chair Person got his way over the new chair, more or less. The men carried it to the garden shed and shoved it inside. Then they left, looking almost as bewildered and angry as Dad.

Marcia, watching and listening, was quite sure now that Chair Person had been learning from Auntie Christa all these years. He knew just how to make people do what he wanted. But Auntie Christa did not live in the house. You could escape from her sometimes. Chair Person seemed to be here to stay.

"We'll have to get him turned back into a chair somehow," she said to Simon. "He's not getting better. He's getting worse and worse."

Simon found he agreed. He was not sorry for Chair Person at all now. "Yes, but *how* do we turn him back?" he said.

Chapter Five

"We could ask old Mr Pennyfeather," Marcia suggested. "The conjuring set came from his shop."

So that afternoon they left Mum lying on her bed upstairs and Dad moodily picking up frost-bitten apples from the grass. Chair Person was still eating lunch in the kitchen.

"Where does he put it all?" Marcia wondered as they hurried down the road.

"He's a chair. He's got lots of room for stuffing," Simon pointed out.

Then they both said, "Oh *no*!" Chair Person was blundering up the road after them, panting and snuffling and waving his arms. "Er, hn hm, wait for me!" he called out. "You appear to have snuffle left me behind."

He tramped beside them, looking pleased with himself. When they got to the shops where all the people were, shoppers turned to stare as Chair Person clumped past in Dad's shoes. Their eyes went from the shoes, to the football socks, and then to the short, striped suit, and then on up to stare wonderingly at the smashed-hedgehog beard. More heads turned every time Chair Person's voice brayed out, and of course he talked a lot. There was something in every shop to set him going.

At the bread shop, he said, "Er, hn hm, those are Sam Browne's Homebaked loaves. I happen to know snuffle they are nutrition for the nation."

Outside the supermarket, he said, "Cheese to please, you can snuffle freeze it squeeze it and – er, hn hm – there is Tackley's Tea which I happen to know has over a thousand holes to every bag. Flavour to snuffle savour."

Outside the wine shop his voice went up to a high roar. "I – hn hm – see Sampa's Superb Sherry here which is for ladies who like everything silky snuffle smooth. And I happen to know that in the black bottle there is – hn hm – a taste of Olde England. There is a stagecoach on the – hn hm – label to prove it. And look, there is Bogan's – hn hm – Beer which is of course for Only The Best."

By now it seemed to Simon and Marcia that everyone in the street was staring. "You don't want to believe everything the ads say," Simon said uncomfortably.

"Er, hn hm, I appear to be making you feel embarrassed," Chair Person brayed, louder than ever. "Just tell me snuffle if I am in your way and I will snuffle go home."

"Yes, do," they both said.

"I – er, hn hm – wouldn't dream of pushing in where I am snuffle not wanted," Chair Person said. "I would – hn hm – count it a favour if you tell me snuffle truthfully every time you've had enough of me. I – er, hn hm – know I must bore you quite often."

By the time he had finished saying this they had arrived at old Mr Pennyfeather's junk shop. Chair Person stared at it.

"We – er, hn hm – don't need to go in there," he said. "Everything in it is old."

"You can stay outside then," said Marcia.

But Chair Person went into another long speech about not wanting to be – hn hm – a trouble to them and followed them into the shop. “I – er, hn hm – might get lost,” he said, “and then what would you do?”

He bumped into a cupboard.

Its doors opened with a *clap* and a stream of horse shoes poured out: clatter, *clatter*, CLATTER!

Chair Person lurched sideways from the horse shoes and walked into an umbrella stand made out of an elephant’s foot, which fell over – *crash*, CLATTER – against a coffee table with a big jug on it, which tipped and slid the jug off – CRASH, splinter, splinter – and then fell against a rickety bookcase, which collapsed sideways, spilling books – thump, thump, thump-thump-thump – and hit another table loaded with old magazines and music, which all poured down around Chair Person.

It was like dominoes going down.

The bell at the shop door had not stopped ringing before Chair Person was surrounded by knocked-over furniture and knee-deep in old papers. He stood in the midst of them, waving his arms and looking injured.

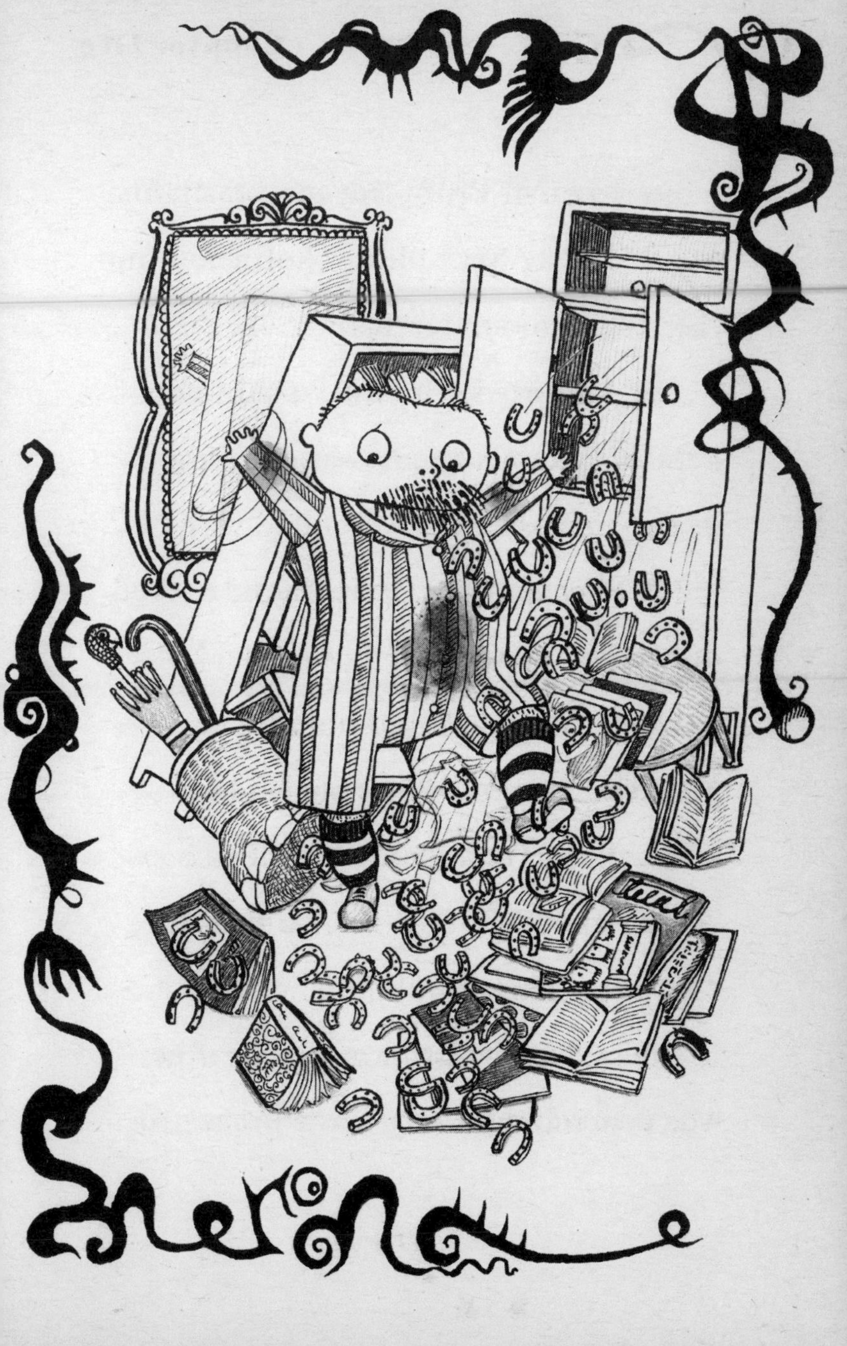

Chapter Five

By then, Mr Pennyfeather was on his way from the back of the shop, shouting, "Steady, steady, steady!"

"Er, hn hm – er, hn hm," said Chair Person, "I appear to have knocked one or two things over."

Mr Pennyfeather stopped and looked at him, in a knowing, measuring kind of way. Then he looked at Simon and Marcia. "He yours?" he said. They nodded. Mr Pennyfeather nodded too. "Don't move," he said to Chair Person. "Stay just where you are."

Chair Person's arms waved as if he was conducting a very large orchestra, several massed choirs and probably a brass band or so as well. "I – er, hn hm, er, hn hm – I – er, hn hm –" he began.

Mr Pennyfeather shouted at him. "*Stand still! Don't move, or I'll have the springs out of you and straighten them for toasting forks*! It's the only language they understand," he said to Simon and Marcia. "STAND STILL! YOU HEARD ME!" he shouted at Chair Person.

Chair Person stopped waving his arms and stood like a statue, looking quite frightened.

"You two come this way with me," said Mr Pennyfeather, and he took Simon and Marcia down to the far end of his shop, between an old ship's wheel and a carved maypole, where there was an old radio balanced on a tea chest. He turned the radio up loud so that Chair Person could not hear them. "Now," he said, "I see you two got problems to do with that old conjuring set. What happened?"

"It was Auntie Christa's fault," said Marcia.

"She let the crystal ball drip on the chair," said Simon.

"*And* tapped it with the magic wand," said Marcia.

Mr Pennyfeather scratched his

withered old cheek. "My fault, really," he said. "I should never have let her have those conjuring things, only I'd got sick of the way the stuff in my shop would keep getting lively. Tables dancing and such. Mind you, most of my furniture only got a drip or so. They used to calm down after a couple of hours. That one of yours looks like he got a right old dousing – or maybe the wand helped. What was he to begin with, if you don't mind my asking?"

"Our old armchair," said Simon.

"Really?" said Mr Pennyfeather. "I'd have said he was a sofa, from the looks of him. Maybe what you had was an armchair with a sofa opinion of itself. That happens."

"Yes, but how can we turn him *back*?" said Marcia.

Mr Pennyfeather scratched his withered cheek again. "This is *it*," he said. "Quite a problem. The answer must be in that conjuring set. It wouldn't make no sense to have that crystal ball full of stuff to make things lively without having the antidote close by. That top hat never got lively. You could try tapping him with the wand again. But you'd do well to sort through the box and see if you couldn't come up with whatever was put on the top hat to stop it getting lively at all."

"But we haven't got the box," said Simon. "Auntie Christa's got it."

"Then you'd better borrow it back off her quick," Mr Pennyfeather said, peering along his shop to where Chair Person was still standing like a statue. "Armchairs with big opinions of themselves aren't no good. That one could turn out a real menace."

"He already *is*," said Simon.

Marcia took a deep grateful breath and said, "Thanks awfully, Mr

Pennyfeather. Do you want us to help you tidy up your shop?"

"No, you run along," said Mr Pennyfeather. "I want him out of here before he does any worse." And he shouted down the shop at Chair Person, "Right, you can move now! Out of my shop *at* the double and wait in the street!"

Chair Person nodded and bowed in his most crawlingly humble way and waded through the papers and out of the shop. Simon and Marcia followed, wishing they could manage to shout at Chair Person the way Mr Pennyfeather had. But maybe they had been brought up to be too polite. Or maybe it was Chair Person's sofa opinion of himself. Or maybe it was just that Chair Person was bigger than they were and had offered to eat them when he first came out of the shed. Whatever it was, all they seemed to be able to do was to let Chair Person clump along beside them, talking and talking, and try to think how to turn him into a chair again.

They were so busy thinking that they had turned into their own road before they heard one thing Chair Person said. And that was only because he said something new.

"*What* did you say?" said Marcia.

"I said," said Chair Person, "I appear – er, hn hm, snuffle – to have set fire to your house."

Both their heads went up with a jerk. Sure enough, there was a fire engine standing in the road by their gate. Firemen were dashing about unrolling hoses. Thick black smoke was rolling up from behind the house, darkening the sunlight and turning their roof black.

Simon and Marcia forgot about Chair Person and ran.

Mum and Dad, to their great relief, were standing in the road beside the fire engine, along with most of the neighbours. Mum saw them. She let go of Dad's arm and rushed up to Chair Person.

"All right. Let's have it," she said. "What did you do *this* time?"

Chair Person made bowing and hand-waving movements, but he did not seem sorry or worried. In fact, he was looking up at the surging clouds of black smoke rather smugly. "I – er, hn hm – was thirsty," he said. "I appear to have drunk all your orange juice and lemon squash and the stuff snuffle from the wine and whisky bottles, so I – hn hm – put the kettle on the gas for a cup of tea. I appear to have forgotten it when I went out."

"You fool!" Mum screamed at him. "It was an electric kettle, anyway!" She was angry enough to behave just like Mr Pennyfeather. She pointed a finger at Chair Person's stomach. "I've had enough of you!" she shouted. "You stand there and don't *dare* move! Don't *stir*, or I'll – I'll – I don't know what I'll do but you won't like it!"

And it worked, just like it did when Mr Pennyfeather shouted. Chair Person stood still as an overstuffed statue. "I – hn hm – appear to have annoyed you," he said in his most crawlingly humble way.

Chapter Five

He stood stock still in the road all the time the firemen were putting out the fire. Luckily only the kitchen was burning. Dad had seen the smoke while he was picking up apples in the garden. He had been in time to phone the Fire Brigade and get Mum from the upstairs before the rest of the house caught fire. The firemen hosed the blaze out quite quickly. Half an hour later, Chair Person was still standing in the road and the rest of them were looking round at the ruined kitchen.

Mum gazed at the melted cooker, the crumpled fridge and the charred stump of the kitchen table. Everything was black and wet. The vinyl floor had bubbled. "Someone get rid of Chair Person," Mum said, "before I murder him."

"Don't worry. We're going to," Simon said soothingly.

"But we have to go and help at Auntie Christa's Children's party in order to do it," Marcia explained.

"I'm not going," Mum said. "There's enough to do here – and I'm not doing another thing for Auntie Christa – not after this morning!"

"Even Auntie Christa can't expect us to help at her party after our house has been on fire," Dad said.

"Simon and I will go," Marcia said. "And we'll take Chair Person and get him off your hands."

Chapter Six

The smoke had made everything in the house black and gritty. Simon and Marcia could not find any clean clothes, but the next door neighbours let them use their bathroom and kindly shut up their dog so that Marcia would not feel nervous. The neighbours the other side invited them to supper when they came back. Everyone was very kind. More kind neighbours were standing anxiously round Chair Person when Simon and Marcia came to fetch him. Chair Person was still standing like a statue in the road.

"Is he ill?" the lady from Number 27 asked.

"No, he's not," Marcia said. "He's just eccentric. The Vicar says so."

Simon did his very best to imitate Mr Pennyfeather. "Right," he barked at

Chair Person. "You can move now. We're going to a party."

Though Simon sounded to himself just like a nervous person talking loudly, Chair Person at once started snuffling and waving his arms about. "Oh – hn hm – good," he said. "I believe I shall like a party. What snuffle party is it? Conservative, labour or that party whose name keeps changing? Should I be – hn hm – sick of the moon or over the parrot?"

At this, all the neighbours nodded to one another. "*Very* eccentric," the lady from Number 27 said as they all went away.

Simon and Marcia led Chair Person towards the Community Hall trying to explain that it was a party for The Society for Underprivileged Children. "And we're supposed to be helping," Marcia said. "So do you think you could try to behave like a proper person for once?"

"You – hn hm – didn't have to say *that*!" Chair Person said. His feelings were hurt. He followed them into the hall in silence.

The hall was quite nicely decorated with bunches of balloons and full of children. Simon and Marcia knew most of the children from school. They were surprised they were underprivileged – most of them seemed just ordinary children. But the thing they looked at mostly was the long table at the other end of the room. It had a white cloth on it. Much of it was covered with food: jellies, cakes, crisps and big bottles of fizzy pop. But at one end was the pile of prizes, with the green teddy on top. The conjuring set, being quite big, was at the bottom of the pile. Simon and Marcia were glad, because that would mean it would be the last prize anybody won. They would have time to look through the box.

Auntie Christa was in the midst of the children, trying to pin someone's torn dress. "There you are at last!" she called to Simon and Marcia. "Where are your mother and father?"

"They couldn't come – we're awfully sorry!" Marcia called back.

Auntie Christa rushed out from among the children. "Couldn't come? Why *not*?" she said.

"Our house has been on fire —" Simon began to explain.

But Auntie Christa, as usual, did not listen. "I think that's extremely thoughtless of them!" she said. "I was counting on them to run the games. Now I shall have to run them myself."

While they were talking, Chair Person lumbered into the crowd of children, waving his arms importantly. "Er, hn hm, welcome to the party," he brayed. "You are all honoured to have me here because I am – snuffle – Chair Person and you are only children who are underprivileged."

The children stared at him resentfully. None of them thought of themselves as underprivileged. "Why is he wearing football socks?" someone asked.

Auntie Christa whirled round and

stared at Chair Person. Her face went quite pale. "Why did you bring *him*?" she said.

"He – er – he needs looking after," Marcia said, rather guiltily.

"He just nearly burnt our house down," Simon tried to explain again.

But Auntie Christa did not listen. "I shall speak to your mother very crossly indeed!" she said and ran back among the children, clapping her hands. "Now listen, children. We are going to play a lovely game. Stand quiet while I explain the rules."

"Er, hn hm," said Chair Person. "There

appears to be a feast laid out over there. Would it snuffle trouble you if I started eating it?"

At this, quite a number of the children called out, "Yes! Can we eat the food now?"

Auntie Christa stamped her foot. "No you may *not*! Games come first. All of you stand in a line and Marcia bring those hacky sacks from over there."

Once Auntie Christa started giving orders, Chair Person became quite obedient. He did his best to join in the games. He was hopeless. It someone threw him a hacky sack, he dropped it. If he threw a hacky sack at someone else, it hit the wall or threatened to land in a jelly. The team he was in lost every time.

So Auntie Christa tried team Follow My Leader and that was even worse. Chair Person lost the team he was with and galumphed round in small circles on his own. Then he noticed that everyone was running in zig-zags and ran in zig-zags too. He zagged when everyone else zigged, bumping into people and treading on toes.

"Can't you stop him? He's spoiling the *game*!" children kept complaining.

Luckily, Chair Person kept drifting off

to the table to steal buns or help himself to a pint or so of fizzy pop. After a while, Auntie Christa stopped rounding him up back into the games. It was easier without him.

But Simon and Marcia were getting worried. They were being kept so busy helping with teams and fetching things and watching in case people cheated that they had no time at all to get near the conjuring set. They watched the other prizes go. The green teddy was first, then the broken train, and then other things, until half the pile was gone.

Then at last Auntie Christa said the

next game was Musical Chairs. “Simon and Marcia will work the record player and I’ll be the judge,” she said. “All of you bring one chair each into the middle. *And* you!” she said, grabbing Chair Person away from where he was trying to eat a jelly. “This is a game even you can play.”

“Good,” Simon whispered as he and Marcia went over to the ancient record player. “We can look in the box while the music’s going.”

Marcia picked up an old scratched record and set it on the turntable. “I thought we were never going to get a chance!" she said. "We can give them a good long go with the music first time." She carefully lowered the lopsided needle. The record began:

Here we go gathering click *in May,* click *in May, nuts in* click... and all the children danced cautiously round the chairs, with Chair Person prancing in their midst, waving his arms like a lobster.

Simon and Marcia ran to the table and pulled the conjuring box out from under the other prizes. The crystal ball was still leaking. There was quite a damp patch on the tablecloth. But the wand was lying on top when they opened the box, still wrapped in flags. Simon snatched it up. Marcia ran back and lifted the needle off the record. There was a stampede for chairs.

Chair Person of course was the one without a chair. Simon had expected that. He followed Chair Person and gave him a smart tap with the wand as Chair Person blundered up the line of sitting children. But the wand did not seem to work. Chair Person pushed the smallest girl off the end chair and sat in it himself.

"I saw that! You were out!" Auntie Christa shouted, pointing at him.

Chair Person sat where he was. "I – er, hn hm – appear to be sitting in a chair," he said. "That was the snuffle rule as I understand it."

Auntie Christa glared. "Start the game again," she said.

Simon tapped Chair Person on the head with the wand before everyone got up, but that did not seem to work either. "What shall we *do*?" he whispered to Marcia, as they hurried back to the record player.

"Try it without the flags," Marcia whispered back. She lowered the needle again.

Here we go gathering click *in May*, the record began as Simon dashed over to the table, unwrapping the string of flags from the wand as he went. He was just putting the flags back in the box, when the table gave a sort of wriggle and stamped one of its legs.

Simon beckoned Marcia madly. The box must have been standing on the table for quite a long time. The stuff from the crystal ball had leaked down into the table and spread along the tablecloth to the food. The tablecloth was rippling itself, in a sly, lazy way. As Marcia arrived, one of the jellies spilt its way up to the edge of its bowl and peeped timidly out.

"It's *all* getting lively," Simon said.

"We'd better take the crystal ball to the toilet and drain it away," Marcia said.

"No!" said Simon. "Think what might happen if the toilet gets lively! Think of something else."

"Why should *I* always have to be the one to think?" Marcia snapped. "Get an idea for yourself for once!" She knew this was unfair, but by this time she was in as bad a fuss as Mum.

Here the record got as far as *who shall*

we click *to* click *him away*? and stuck. *Who shall we* click, *who shall we* click...

Marcia raced for the record and took it off. Simon raced among the stampede towards Chair Person and hit him with the unwrapped wand. Again nothing happened. Chair Person pushed a boy with a plaster cast on his leg off the end chair and sat down. Auntie Christa said angrily, "This is *too* bad! Start the game again."

Marcia put the needle down on the beginning of the record a third time. "I'd better stay and do this," she said. "You'd better go and search the box – quickly, before we get landed with Table Person and Jelly Person as well!"

Simon sped to the table and started taking things out of the conjuring box – first the flags, then the dripping hat with the crystal ball in it. After that came a toy rabbit, which was perhaps meant to be lively when it was fetched out of the hat. Yet, for some reason, it was just a toy. None of the things in the box was more than just wet. Simon took out a sopping pack of cards, and a dripping bundle of coloured handkerchiefs. They were all just ordinary. That meant that there *had* to be a way of stopping things getting lively, but search as he would, Simon could not find it.

As he searched, the cracked music stopped and started and the table stamped one leg after another in time to it. Simon glanced at the game. Chair Person had found another way to cheat. He simply sat in his chair the whole time.

"I'm counting you out," Auntie Christa kept saying. And Chair Person went on sitting there with his smashed-hedgehog beard pointing obstinately to the ceiling.

Next time Simon looked, there were only two chairs left beside Chair Person's and three children. "We'll have tea after this game," Auntie Christa called as Marcia started the music again.

Help! thought Simon. The wobbling, climbing jelly was half out of its bowl, waving little feelers. Simon turned the whole box out on to the dancing table. All sorts of things fell out. But there was nothing he could see that looked useful – except perhaps a small wet box. There was a typed label on its lid that said DISAPPEARING BOX. Simon hurriedly opened it.

It was empty inside, so very empty that he could not see the bottom. Simon put it down on the table and stared into it, puzzled.

Just then, the table got livelier than ever from all the liquid Simon had emptied out of the conjuring box. It started to dance properly. The tablecloth got quite lively too and stretched itself in a long, lazy ripple. The two things together rolled the hat with the crystal ball in it across the tiny, empty box.

There was a soft WHOP. The hat and the crystal ball were sucked into the box. And they were gone. Just like that. Simon stared.

The table was still dancing and the

tablecloth was still rippling. One by one, and very quickly, the other things from the conjuring box were rolled and jogged across the tiny box. WHOP went the rabbit, WHOP the wand, WHOP-WHOP the string of flags, and then all the other

things WHOP WHOP WHOP, and they were all gone too. The big box that had held the things tipped over and made a bigger WHOP. And that was gone as well, before Simon could move. After that the other prizes started to vanish, WHOP WHOP WHOP. This seemed to interest the tablecloth. It put out a long exploring corner towards the box.

At that, Simon came to his senses. He pushed the corner aside and rammed the lid on the box before the tablecloth had a chance to vanish too.

As soon as the lid was on, the box was not there any more. There was not even a whisper of a WHOP as it went. It was just gone. And the tablecloth was just a tablecloth, lying half wrapped across the few prizes left. And the table stood still and was just a table. The jelly slid back into its bowl. Its feelers were gone and it was just a jelly.

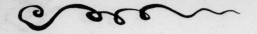

The music stopped too. Auntie Christa stopped too. Auntie Christa called out, "Well done, Philippa! You've won again! Come and choose a prize, dear."

"It's not fair!" somebody else complained. "Philippa's won *everything*!"

Marcia came racing over to Simon as he tried to straighten the tablecloth.

"Look, look! You *did* it! Look!"

Simon turned round in a dazed way. There were still two chairs standing in the middle of the hall after the game. One of them was an old shabby striped armchair. Simon was sure that was not right. "Who put—?" he began. Then he noticed that the chair was striped in sky-blue, orange and purple. Its stuffing was leaking in a sort of fuzz from its sideways top cushion. It had stains on both arms and on the seat. Chair Person was a chair again. The only odd thing was that the chair was wearing football socks and shiny shoes on its two front legs.

"I'm not sure if it was the wand or the box," Simon said.

They pushed the armchair over

against the wall while everyone was crowding round the food.

"I don't think I could bear to have it on our bonfire after this," Marcia said. "It wouldn't seem quite kind."

"If we take its shoes and socks off," Simon said, "we could leave it here. People will probably think it belongs to the hall."

"Yes, it would be quite useful here," Marcia agreed.

Later on, after the children had gone and Auntie Christa had locked up the hall, saying over her shoulder, "Tell your mother and father that I'm not on speaking terms with either of them!"

Simon and Marcia walked slowly home.

Simon asked, "Do you think he knew we were going to put him on our bonfire? Was he having his revenge on us?"

"He may have been," said Marcia. "He never talked about the bonfire, did he? But what was to stop him just *asking* us not to when he was a person?"

"No," said Simon. "He didn't have to set the house on fire. I suppose that shows the kind of Person he was."

Angus Flint

Tony, Candida and Pip

Pip

Angus driving

Menace

Chair Person

Marcia and Simon

The chair

Mum

If you liked VILE VISITORS, you'll love:

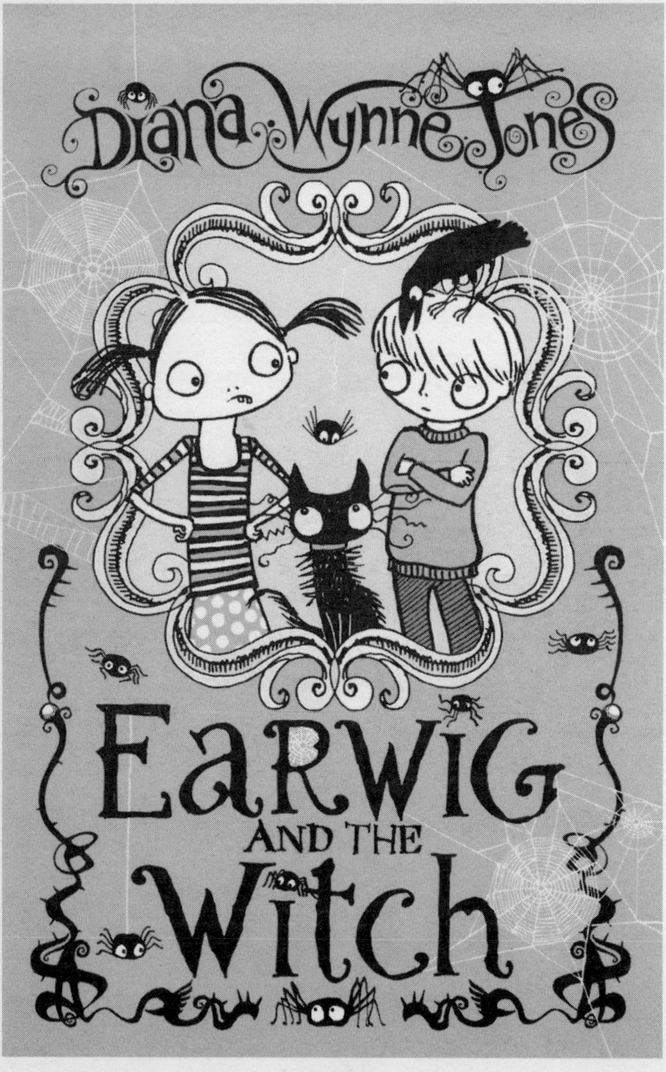